World of Reading

LEVEL 2

GAME OVER

Written by Nancy Lambert

Illustrated by Ron Lim *and* Rachelle Rosenberg

Based on the Marvel comic book series Ant-Man

MARVEL
Los Angeles
New York

Printed in the United States of America
First Edition, October 2015
1 3 5 7 9 10 8 6 4 2
FAC-029261-15247
ISBN 978-1-4847-3130-7
Library of Congress Control Number: 2015910896

Ant-Man has cool super powers.
He can shrink really small
or call ants to help him.

Cassie is Ant-Man's daughter.
Cassie thinks her dad's powers
are so cool.

Ant-Man takes Cassie to
the video game arcade.
Cassie loves pinball machines!

Then Ant-Man and Cassie
eat ice cream cones.

It is time for Cassie to do
her homework. Cassie forgot her
backpack at the arcade!
The arcade is closed.
Cassie's backpack is locked inside.

Ant-Man is not worried.
He has a great idea!
He can shrink them both!

Ant-Man shrinks himself and
Cassie down to the size of ants.

Ant-Man and Cassie are very small. They can just walk under the arcade door.

The video game arcade is quiet.
Everything is turned off.

Cassie finds her backpack.
Ant-Man shrinks it down, too.
They are ready to leave.

Ant-Man has another great idea.
They are small enough to fit
inside the pinball games.

Ant-Man and Cassie can walk inside the games.

They are very small.
Everything looks huge!

Ant-Man and Cassie climb into a space robot game.

They stroll over glow-in-the-dark stars. They walk through a giant robot's eye.

Ant-Man and Cassie crawl into a mermaid game. They spot shiny shells. Cassie spies a mermaid!

Ant-Man and Cassie climb into a circus game. They see animals and a big clown face.

Then Ant-Man and Cassie climb
into a haunted house game.

They see creepy cobwebs and spooky ghosts. There are traps and tricks everywhere.

Cassie falls through a trapdoor!
She falls into a deep hole.

Cassie can't climb out, and
Ant-Man can't reach her!

Cassie slides deeper into the hole.
Ant-Man calls the ants to help him.

Many ants hear when Ant-Man calls. They hurry to the arcade.

The ants meet Ant-Man by the hole.
They will help save Cassie!

The flying ants are too big to fit in the hole. The smaller ants are too tiny to reach Cassie alone.

Ant-Man has a great idea! He asks the small ants to work together.

The ants cling to each other to make a ladder. Cassie climbs up the ant ladder.

Cassie is safe!
Ant-Man and Cassie thank the ants.

They leave the video game arcade.
Ant-Man makes himself big again.
He makes Cassie big again, too.

From now on, Ant-Man and Cassie will play pinball only from outside the games.